Y0-BYU-216

To:

From:

What Would Jane Do?

By Heather Zschock

Illustrated by Marilena Perilli

PETER PAUPER PRESS, INC.
White Plains, New York

With lots of love
for Martha

The text in this book consists of fictional statements and fanciful reactions of the women mentioned. They are based on the imagination of the author and several helpful friends.

Illustrations copyright © 2005 Marilena Perilli
www.artscounselinc.com

Designed by Heather Zschock

Copyright © 2005
Peter Pauper Press, Inc.
202 Mamaroneck Avenue
White Plains, NY 10601

ISBN 0-88088-505-X
Printed in China
7 6 5 4 3 2 1

Visit us at www.peterpauper.com

What Would Jane Do?

Every now and then,
life throws us a curveball,
a run in our stockings,
or a few extra pounds.

Don't despair!

In the face of life's challenges, we must seek the advice and guidance of other women who have been THERE before (wherever "there" is). Put yourself in their party shoes and imagine how they might react to YOUR sticky situation.

Remember, there actually IS a light at the end of the tunnel, and more important, you are not alone.

What would Jackie Kennedy do?

Put on a great pair of shades, and face the world with her head held high.

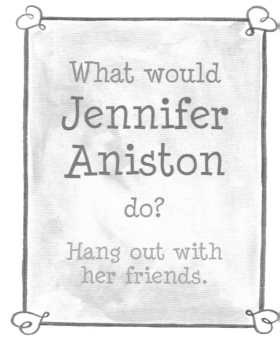

What would
Cinderella
do?

Show up at
the ball and
dance with
the prince.

What would **Mona Lisa** do?

Smile mysteriously.

What would

Holly
Golightly
do?

Have breakfast
at Tiffany's.

What would

Jackie
Joyner-
Kersee

do?

Run like the wind.

What would

Athena

do?

Find her
inner goddess.

What would

Barbara

Walters do?

Ask all the right questions.

What would

Demi

Moore do?

Look fabulous and date a younger man.

What would
Jane Eyre
do?

Marry her boss.

What would
Super
Woman
do?

Put on a form-fitting outfit
and save the day.

What would
Connie
Chung
do?

Be well-informed.

What would
Betty
Crocker
do?

Stir things up.

What would
Eve
do?

Be the first.

What would
**Grandma
Moses**
do?

Start a new career
(at any age).

What would

the Statue of Liberty do?

Carry a torch
for freedom.

What would **Aretha Franklin** do?

Demand R-E-S-P-E-C-T.

What would
Annie
do?

Look forward
to tomorrow.

What would
Jane
Austen do?

Live with neither pride nor prejudice.

What would

Julie
Andrews

do?

Follow every rainbow
'til she finds her dream.

What would
Julia
Roberts
do?

Be a Pretty Woman.

What would

Gilda
Radner

do?

Laugh it off on
a Saturday Night.

What would
Farrah Fawcett
do?

Be an angel.

What would
Lady
Godiva
do?
Have another bon bon.

What would

Ruth Bader

Ginsburg

do?

Be a good

judge of character.

What would
Nancy
Drew do?

Follow the clues.

What would Susan B. Anthony do?

Cast her vote.

What would **Katharine Graham** do?

Post the news.

What would
Little Miss
Muffet
do?
Squash the spider.

What would
Marilyn Monroe
do?

Go platinum.

What would

Gloria
Gaynor

do?

Change the stupid locks.

What would

Helen of

Troy

do?

Launch a thousand ships.

What would

Estée
Lauder

do?

Put her best face forward.

What would

Carrie

Bradshaw

(from *Sex and the City*)

do?

Buy a new pair of shoes.

What would

Billie Holiday

do?

Call the whole thing off.

What would

Mia
Hamm

do?

Reach her goals.

What would

Betsy Ross

do?

Sew up the
loose ends.

What would
Cyndi
Lauper
do?

Have fun.

What would
Annika
Sorenstam
do?
Give it her best shot.

What would

Agatha
Christie

do?

Find out whodunnit.

What would

Rosa
Parks
do?

Not take a back
seat to anyone.

What would
Indira
Gandhi
do?
Keep
the peace.

What would

Sacagawea

do?

Explore a
new frontier.

What would

Scarlett O'Hara

do?

Remember that tomorrow is another day.

What would

Lillian
Gish

do?

Take a bow.

What would

Pat

(from *Saturday Night Live*)

do?

Make gender
a non-issue.

What would

Dorothy

do?

Go home.

What would

Lucille
Ball

do?

Create havoc with
her best friend.

What would

Annie Oakley

do?

Be a straight shooter.

What would

Oprah
Winfrey

do?

Overcome adversity.

What would
Sleeping

Take a good long nap.

Beauty do?

What would

Coco
Chanel

do?

Leave them in stitches.

What would
Sally
Ride
do?

Shoot for the moon.

What would

Mary Tyler Moore

do?

do?

Turn the world on

with her smile.

What would

Picabo
Street

do?

Go for the gold.

What would
Madonna
do?

Strike a pose.

What would

Barbra
Streisand

do?

Be a Funny Girl.

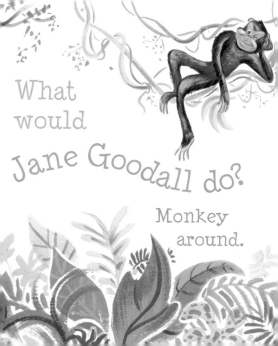

What
would

Jane Goodall do?

Monkey
around.

What would

Hillary
Clinton

do?

Upstage her husband.